Erin Rafanello Ferguson is someone who is very passionate about event planning, as well as writing, and decided to merge both of them a few years ago. She began freelancing for a newspaper publication regarding arts and entertainment, with a focus on celebrity and local talent. Her love for holidays and writing led her to the path of becoming an author after cutting down a Christmas tree that had some spiders in it. Softening the blow of these unfortunate houseguests was her main focus, as well as the way Earl emerged with the help of her two little girls, Sawyer and Harlan.

Earl:
The Christmas Tree Spider
Erin Rafanello Ferguson

AUSTIN MACAULEY PUBLISHERS™
LONDON * CAMBRIDGE * NEW YORK * SHARJAH

Copyright © Erin Rafanello Ferguson 2019

Ordering Information:
Quantity sales: special discounts are available on quantity purchases by corporations, associations, and others. For details, contact the publisher at the address below.

Publisher's Cataloging-in-Publication data
Ferguson, Erin Rafanello
Earl: The Christmas Tree Spider

ISBN 9781643781433 (Paperback)
ISBN 9781643781440 (Hardback)
ISBN 9781645367062 (ePub e-book)

Library of Congress Control No: 2019908441

The main category of the book — JUVENILE FICTION / Holidays & Celebrations / Christmas & Advent

www.austinmacauley.com/us

First Published 2019
Austin Macauley Publishers LLC
40 Wall Street, 33rd Floor, Suite 3302
New York, NY 10005
USA

mail-usa@austinmacauley.com
+1 (646) 5125767

This book is dedicated to my daughters, Sawyer and Harlan, who inspire me to reach for the stars every day. To my sons, Owen Michael and Nash Ryan, in heaven; your spirits are with us at Christmas and always. To my husband, Jeremy, for his continued support. To my best friend, Erica, without whom I would be lost. And finally to my parents, Ben and Debbie, and grandparents, Henry and Dolores, my angels in heaven.

It was a cold winter day, and Earl was in search of a wonderful tree he could call home.
While walking through the forest, he stumbled upon a field of beautiful evergreen trees. There were rows and rows of Douglas Firs, Noble Firs, Frasier Firs, and Noble Kings, when all of a sudden he saw the most beautiful tree he had ever seen.

"There it is! That's my tree! That's my new home! It's meant to be," said Earl loudly.

Earl ran as fast as he could and took a leap onto the tree. He ran up and down and all around, and was so excited he had found a place to call his own just in time for Christmas.

"This is going to be great. I can't wait to hang my stocking and light the tree, snuggle up with some hot cocoa, and sing songs with glee," Earl said.

As he began setting up his cozy little bed and rocking chair on one of the branches, Earl began to sing, "Oh Christmas tree! Oh Christmas tree…" when suddenly his home, the tree, began to shake.

"Oh no," cried Earl. Scared, he ran and hid under his bed.

BOOM! The tree went crashing to the ground, but Earl couldn't move. He was too scared to look and see what was happening. He could feel the wind getting stronger and stronger, and just held on tight, hoping he wouldn't fly away. Finally, the wind stopped, but the shaking then continued until *BOOM*…and all was still.

"My goodness!" said Earl. "What just happened?"

He crawled out from under his bed, slowly calmed down, and began to get settled into his new home again, when he noticed lights and laughter.

What is going on, thought Earl. He peeked out and saw a family. They were laughing and singing Christmas songs while decorating the tree… *It is so nice*, Earl thought to himself, and then he began to sing as well.

As Earl sat there admiring all the festive fun the family was having, he started to get sad, wanting a family of his own. He thought this family would fear him because he was a spider, so he decided to write a letter to Santa.

Dear Santa,

I've been good all year. You can check with your elves, check with them twice, I promise you I have been nice.

I found this tree, a place to call my own, but what I really want is a happy, loving home.

I know I am a spider and they are not, but do you think they would accept me, could we give it a shot?

Please help me make this dream come true, I would really appreciate it if you do.

Love,
Earl

He left his letter on the side table next to his bed and pulled his covers up over his head. He tossed and turned, thinking of how happy he would be with a new family, not just the tree.

Christmas morning arrived, and Earl woke up to a nice surprise. The family saw Earl while decorating the tree and hung a stocking for him on Christmas Eve. He couldn't believe it, but he was so happy, and before he knew it, a tear dropped off his face and out of the tree.

SPLASH! The tear dropped on Henry's foot. "Hello Earl and Merry Christmas," said Henry.

Earl climbed out from inside the tree and said, "Merry Christmas to you too and thank you for my stocking, but how did you know my name?"

"We looked in the tree while you were sleeping and saw it on your stocking that you hung. We wanted you to feel welcome in our home, so we hung one for you as well, among our own."

"Am…am I…a part…of your family?" Earl asked with a trembling voice and big watery eyes.
"Of course!" said Dolores. "Welcome to your new home!"

Earl simply couldn't believe it. He was as happy as he could be. "Thank you, Santa Claus!" said Earl.

A beautiful Christmas tree turned into a home, with a family that accepted Earl and a place to call his own…

So don't fear the little spiders, children, they are just friends in your home.
Merry Christmas!

END.